Mermaids

by Lucille Recht Penner
illustrated by Mel Grant

A STEPPING STONE BOOK™
Random House 🏠 New York

To Leah and Lilly Recht
—L.R.P.

For happy mermaids everywhere.
And to Kaz, the girl with a treacle heart.
—*M.G.*

Text copyright © 2008 by Lucille Recht Penner.
Illustrations copyright © 2008 by Mel Grant.

All rights reserved.
Published in the United States by Random House Children's Books, a division
of Random House, Inc., New York.

Random House and colophon are registered trademarks and A Stepping
Stone Book and colophon are trademarks of Random House, Inc.

www.steppingstonesbooks.com
www.randomhouse.com/kids
www.melgrant.com

Educators and librarians, for a variety of teaching tools, visit us at
www.randomhouse.com/teachers

Library of Congress Cataloging-in-Publication Data
Penner, Lucille Recht.
Mermaids / by Lucille Recht Penner ; illustrated by Mel Grant. — 1st ed.
    p.   cm.
"A stepping stone book."
ISBN 978-0-375-83936-8 (pbk.) — ISBN 978-0-375-93936-5 (lib. bdg.)
1. Mermaids—Juvenile literature.   I. Grant, Melvyn, ill.   II. Title.
GR910.P36 2008   398.21—dc22   2007021741

Printed in the United States of America

10 9 8 7 6 5 4 3 2

First Edition

Contents

1
The Mermaid Myth

Sun sparkles on the water. A beautiful woman sits on a rock that rises from the sea. She is combing her long hair. In one hand, she holds a mirror with a pearl handle.

Suddenly there is a shout from the shore. Someone has seen her! The woman quickly dives into the waves. She vanishes with a flip of her silvery tail.

Her tail? Yes. This lovely creature is a mermaid. Instead of legs, she has a fish tail. And her home is deep in the sea.

You can't find a mermaid at a zoo. Aquariums don't have them. There aren't any in museums. But many people have said they have seen them.

One of those people was Christopher

Columbus. In 1493, he was sailing off the coast of Haiti when his crew spotted three mermaids. Columbus took a look. "They are not so beautiful as they are painted," he wrote in his journal.

Captain John Smith, whose life was saved by the Indian princess Pocahontas, said he saw a mermaid, too. It happened

while he was sailing to America. She had "a finely shaped nose," he said, "well-formed ears, and green hair."

Were these famous men just making up stories? Or did they see something that *looked* like a mermaid?

Some people may have seen a weird sea animal—the manatee. What a strange mistake to make! Manatees are big and plain-looking. They are often called sea cows.

But mistakes can easily happen. Maybe the light was dim. Or maybe it was raining.

Manatees are mammals. That means a mother manatee feeds her baby with milk. She raises herself and the baby partly out of the water. From far away, she might look like a woman holding a baby. If something scares her, she dives under the water. She even flips up her tail like a mermaid.

When somebody thought that he saw a mermaid, he told everyone he knew. And they told other people. The story spread quickly. People who hadn't seen mermaids believed that *other* people had.

Besides, mermaids didn't seem so odd. People believed in even stranger beasts, like elephants and giraffes. Most people had never seen an elephant or giraffe, either. So why not believe in a woman who was half fish?

2
Scary Mermaids

A mermaid's song is the loveliest sound in the world. When you hear a few notes, you want to get closer. But watch out!

Ancient sailors always worried when they sailed into unknown waters. *Anything* could be hiding in the sea. Old sailing maps showed ugly monsters lurking under the waves. They also showed beautiful mermaids. Sailors feared the mermaids as much as the monsters.

They had good reason. There were many scary mermaids. One kind was a German mermaid, called a nix. She could turn herself into a beautiful girl. On land, she sang and danced.

But that wasn't all a nix could do. She could tell a person what was going to happen in the future. And she was always right. She didn't do it to help people. She did it to make them trust her. Then she lured them into deep water and drowned them.

Other dangerous mermaids lived off

the coast of Norway. They were called the havfine (hahv-FEE-nuh). The havfine drowned many sailors. But sometimes they were merciful.

A fishing boat was sailing home when the wind began to blow hard. Huge waves climbed toward the sky.

A mermaid rose out of the water. Her hands were full of fish.

The sailors were terrified. They had heard stories. If a mermaid threw fish at a boat, the men on board would drown.

The mermaid turned. She threw the fish away *from the boat. The sailors cheered. They would be safe!*

The mermaid slowly sank beneath the waves. The wind stopped blowing and the sea grew calm.

An English mermaid called Jenny Greenteeth lived in lakes and rivers. When the sun went down and the sky turned black, she peeked out. If someone came too close, she reached up and grabbed him.

Jenny was quick. She also had very long arms. In a flash, she pulled her victim under the water. Then she chewed him up with her sharp green teeth.

"Watch out for Jenny!" parents warned their children. *"Don't get too near the water!"*

Jenny Greenteeth wasn't the only mermaid who ate people. There were many, many stories about mermaids eating sailors.

But did *sailors* ever eat *mermaids*?

Sure. In 1739, newspapers reported that English sailors had eaten a mermaid on an island in the Indian Ocean. According to the story, she weighed four hundred pounds and tasted like veal.

3
Amazing Mermaids

Most mermaids were afraid to leave the sea. Bright sun hurt their eyes. It burned their scaly tails.

But they were curious about humans. Sometimes they popped up for a quick look. A few of them used magic to leave the water. They turned their tails into legs and walked on land. Then the sun didn't bother them. Most people thought they were human.

But there *was* a way to tell.

Even on land, a mermaid still had little webs between her fingers. And one

corner of her apron was always wet.

Most mermaids were the size of a human woman. Others were so teeny that they could sleep in clamshells. And some were giants. An old book describes a mermaid who was found on a beach in Scotland. She was 195 feet long!

Many other mermaids have been seen in Scottish waters. In 1688, a Scottish almanac told readers about a special place on the seashore. There they could hear mermaids sing "God Save the King."

People have been telling stories about mermaids from earliest times. In some countries, people worshiped them.

In ancient Syria, traders sailed the wide seas to buy and sell goods. Storms could overturn their small ships in a minute. So they prayed to a mermaid named Atargis (uh-TAR-gis). She was the goddess of the moon and controlled the tides. Atargis could make the seas gentle and safe.

What else could mermaids do? A famous story says that China was founded by a mermaid and her husband, a merman. Before then, people lived like animals. This wonderful couple taught them how to grow plants, build houses, use numbers, read, and write.

Of course, some mermaids could be nice

or mean. You could never be sure which.

The Igbo people of West Africa always watched out for a mermaid named Mami Wata. She kept a python wrapped around her body. The Igbo people had to be careful with Mami Wata. If she was angry, she

drowned the people she met. But if she liked them, she brought them to live in her fabulous palace under the waves.

Japanese mermaids, ningyos (NIN-gyohz), were never mean. They brought good luck to everyone who saw them. It was even luckier if you *ate* a ningyo. Then you would never grow old and die.

But ningyos were very hard to catch. It is unlikely that anyone ever ate one.

There were all kinds of mermaids. Some of them liked people very much. In fact, if a mermaid really, *really* liked you, she might even marry you!

4
Marry Me

Could a man marry a fish? It seemed like a terrible idea. But lots of men wanted to anyway.

Not just any fish, of course. They wanted to marry mermaids.

If a poor man married a mermaid, he might become rich. Over the centuries, thousands of ships have been sunk in battles and storms. All the gold, silver, and jewels on the ocean floor belonged to the mermaids.

Besides being rich, many mermaids were beautiful. They sang like angels. Even when they spoke, it sounded like music was playing. And they were the daughters of

the King and Queen of the Waves. Who
wouldn't want to marry a princess!

Most mermaids didn't wear clothes.
But Irish mermaids, called merrows, wore
magic caps and sealskin cloaks. In fact,
people who saw them swimming often
thought they *were* seals.

A merrow's clothing could get her in trouble. If a man stole her cap or cloak, she couldn't return to the water. She had to marry him.

Once, a man saw a lovely mermaid combing her long green hair. He quickly grabbed her red cap.

The mermaid was terrified. "Are you going to eat me?" she asked.

"Of course not," he said. "I am going to marry you."

The mermaid had to agree. For many years, she was happy with her husband. But one day she found her red cap. Her husband had hidden it in a hole in the wall. She put it

*on and ran back to the sea. The minute she
dove into the waves, the mermaid forgot all
about her husband. He never saw her again.*

Usually a mermaid wife came to live
with her husband. But sometimes the man
came to live in the sea. All he had to do was

jump in. The minute he did, he could
breathe underwater. He could never return
to land. Instead, his wife brought him
anything he wanted from his old home.

One husband became very sad. His wife
tried to cheer him up. She brought him

flowers, and feathers for his pillow. But he still missed his old life. So she brought him his whole town, with all its houses, people, cows, horses, and ducks. All so he wouldn't feel lonely under the sea.

In fact, most mermaids wanted a human husband rather than a merman. Mermen were very ugly. After a mermaid married one, she became ugly, too. And mermaids *hated* being ugly.

5
Merman Magic

A marriage between a mermaid and a man is strange. But a marriage between a merman and a woman is even stranger.

This happened very rarely. When it did, no one knew where the couple went to live. The people of one Irish village say their great-great-grandfathers were mermen. Even when they are far from the sea, these

villagers hear the rushing sound of waves at night. They say it sounds as if they are holding a big seashell to their ears.

Long ago, people thought it was great to have mermen in their families. Mermen had magical powers. Some mermen were gods.

The earliest known merman was Oannes
(oh-AH-nus). He was worshiped by the
ancient Babylonians. Oannes had the body
of a fish. But under his fish's head was the
head of a man. And under his fish's tail,
human feet stuck out. Oannes lived on land
during the day. But he never ate anything

there. When the sun set, he returned to the sea for his dinner. Then he slept underwater until morning.

In ancient Greece, people believed in a water god named Triton. He had a long, fishy tail and carried a seashell that he blew like a trumpet. When he blew softly, the wind eased and the water became calm. But if Triton was angry, he blew the shell loudly. The noise was horrible. Everyone ran away.

All mermen could call up great storms. If a fisherman caught a merman in his net, there was a big fight. The merman made the wind blow hard. He kicked and bit

furiously. The fishing boat often turned
over and the fisherman drowned. Then the
merman chewed through the net and swam
away.

But sometimes the merman didn't get

away. Then he had to give the fisherman a present in return for his freedom.

A long time ago, off the coast of Iceland, a poor fisherman pulled his net from the water. A merman was caught in it!

He carried the merman to his house. His dog came running and the fisherman kicked it. The merman laughed loudly. Then the fisherman tripped over a clump of grass. He cursed it, and the merman laughed again. When the fisherman's wife came out of their little house, he kissed her. The merman laughed louder than ever.

"Why did you laugh?" the fisherman asked.

"I'll tell you if you take me back to the sea," the merman said. So the fisherman did. Then the merman said, "I laughed because you kicked your dog, who loves you. You kissed your wife, who hates you. You cursed a clump of grass that covers a treasure."

The fisherman hurried home to dig up the clump of grass. It was true! Under it was a box full of gold. He showed the gold to his wife but he never trusted her again, and he was always kind to his dog.

Today, people in Iceland still say, *"And then the merman laughed,"* when someone does something foolish.

6
The Mermaid Mummy

In 1842, an amazing rumor began to spread. The Feejee Mermaid was coming to New York!

She wasn't a live mermaid. She was the mummy of a dead one. But people were excited. They would get to see a real mermaid up close.

The mermaid had been captured near

the Fiji Islands. Her body had been made into a mummy in China. Dr. J. Griffin, an English scientist, had bought her from some sailors. He was bringing her to New York on his way back to England.

As soon as Dr. Griffin stepped off the ship, reporters crowded around. They wanted to see the mermaid. Dr. Griffin said no. He wouldn't let anyone gawk at the mermaid. But they kept begging until he let them have a little peek.

Then Dr. Griffin explained why there had to be mermaids. He said that for everything on land, there was something like it in the sea. There were horses on land

and sea horses in the water. There were lions on land and sea lions in the water. There were women and men on land. So *of course* there were mermaids and mermen in the water.

The reporters were thrilled. Yes, they told their readers. This mermaid is real!

Next, the famous circus master P. T.

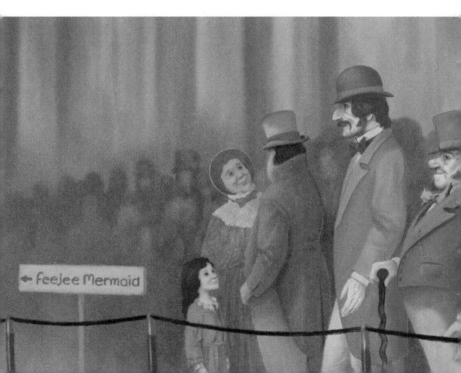

feejee Mermaid

Barnum came to see Dr. Griffin. He asked if he could show the mermaid in his circus. At first, Dr. Griffin said no. But Barnum finally talked him into it.

Barnum advertised the show all over New York City. On opening day, people lined up for blocks. They got a surprise. The mermaid didn't look at all like the

beautiful picture in Barnum's ads. She was dried up and ugly. But no one minded. After all, she *was* a mummy.

Years later, the true story got around. The mummy was a hoax! Someone had sewed the body of a monkey to the tail of a large dried fish to make the mermaid. Dr. J. Griffin was phony, too. He worked for P. T. Barnum. The two of them had fooled New York City.

The Feejee Mermaid was not the first fake mermaid. Or the last. There have been plenty of other fakes. One had the head of an orangutan with a baboon's jaw. Fake skin was stretched all over it. Eyes were

painted on the skin. It doesn't sound as if it would look very real. But it fooled lots of people who already believed in mermaids.

So far, no one has ever found a real mermaid, dead or alive. Does that mean mermaids aren't real? Maybe. But the sea is very wide and deep. It holds many mysteries.

Who knows what might be down there?

People will always watch for mermaids. They'll hurry to the rails of ships. They'll run with a shout to the water's edge. And they'll always wonder—what was it they just saw? Could it have been the flash of a mermaid's shining, silvery tail?